To Jacob

Your stories are important, too!

Love
Jenna O

D1539684

ISBN 978-1-7342186-5-7

Printed in the U.S.A.

First Paperback Edition, November 2019

For my nephews, Cordale II and Takai.

Never forget that your stories are important too.

I Am Me

Written by Trevor D.

Illustrated by Christina Rudenko

I am Jayden.
I am me!

No one can be me.
No, not like me!

Here are my toes...

Here are my fingers...

My skin is brown,

just like
my Dad's...

It's like
my Mom's...

I am pretty cool.
No, I am not shy.

My barber says,
he thinks I am fly.

When I play games,

all I do is win!

And I do not cheat in any game I am in.

Oh, how I love to read!
My Dad shows me how.

And I like songs,
I think I'll sing one now.

And after my bath,
after I have been fed.

Before I close my eyes
and go to bed...

I am Jayden.
I am me!

No one can be me.
No, not like me...

Because I Am Me!

About the Author

Trevor D. is an American writer of books for children, grades K-3. Her debut children's book, I Am Me, introduces the main character, Jayden. This is the first book in the coming series which will feature Jayden as he endeavors through life, from the perspective of an African American boy.

Trevor D. has made fostering literacy her mission. She's recognized that brown and black boys are pulling up the rear when it comes to literacy and she is determined to shift the paradigm, one book at a time. She intends to use her platform to promote and advocate for more attention and focus to be given to fostering a love for reading and writing in African American boys, at the early stages in their academic journeys.

Trevor D. has embarked on a quest to utilize her love for writing to create a space where the under-represented can find books where the characters look like them and share a cultural connection. Her goal is to infuse representation in books that will ignite a passion for reading and promote positive self-images. Her intention is also to empower and inspire brown and black boys to seek to excel in life, in a diversity of areas, and not live into the stereotypes that have been set.

While promoting a love for reading in African American boys, Trevor D. also hopes to give ALL children the gift of being able to see the world through the eyes of others. "The gift of empathy is what allows us the ability to embrace our differences and similarities and use them to make the world a better place."-Trevor D.

CPSIA information can be obtained
at www.ICGtesting.com
Printed in the USA
BVHW021951070120
568868BV00001B/1/P